The Magic Flyswatter
A Superhero Tale of Africa
Retold from the Mwindo Epic

She-Mwindo heard the noise. He went to the house of his favorite wife. He saw the boy and was full of rage. "What is this? Did I not say 'no sons'? Did I not say I would kill him?"

He threw his spear at the baby. Mwindo waved his conga. The spear fell short and stuck in the floor. Mwindo pulled it up. He broke it in two.

She-Mwindo cried out. "*Aieeeeeee!* What kind of child is this?"

Mwindo sang and danced and waved his conga.

> I am Mwindo,
> the one born walking,
> the one born talking.
> O my father, you do not want me.
> O my father, you try to kill me.
> But what can you do against me?

Chapter Books by Aaron Shepard

The Ancient Fantasy Series

#1 ~ The Mountain of Marvels
A Celtic Tale of Magic
Retold from *The Mabinogion*

#2 ~ The Songs of Power
A Northern Tale of Magic
Retold from the *Kalevala*

#3 ~ The Magic Flyswatter
A Superhero Tale of Africa
Retold from the Mwindo Epic

#4 ~ The Monkey King
A Superhero Tale of China
Retold from *The Journey to the West*

#5 ~ The Swan Knight
A Medieval Legend
Retold from Wagner's *Lohengrin*

Other Chapter Books

The Man Who Sang to Ghosts
A Japanese Legend

Timothy Tolliver and the Bully Basher

Ancient Fantasy #3

The Magic Flyswatter

A Superhero Tale of Africa
Retold from the Mwindo Epic

Aaron Shepard

Skyhook Press
Friday Harbor, Washington

Ages 10 and up

Version 1.2

For Dad

Contents

How to Say the Names

These pronunciations are only approximate. To be more accurate, say all vowels as in Spanish or Italian. The letter *o*, for example, is halfway between a long and short *o*. The letter *e* is halfway between a short *e* and a long *a*.

conga	KOHNG-gah
Iyangura	EE-yong-GOO-rah
Kahindo	kah-HEE-'n-do
kikoka	kee-KO-kah
Mwindo	MWEE-'n-do
Nyamurairi	nee-AH-moo-rah-EE-ree
She-Mwindo	shay-MWEE-'n-do
Tubondo	too-BO-'n-do

The storyteller stands beside the fire, swaying, dancing, miming, singing, reciting. With one hand he shakes a gourd rattle, with the other he swings a *conga*—a flyswatter made with a buffalo tail on a wooden handle. Anklet bells tinkle as he moves. Three young men beat a wooden drum with sticks.

Listening to him is a crowd of men, women, and children. They sing along at a song's refrain, they repeat whole lines of the story when he pauses to see if they're paying attention. They encourage him with little shouts, whoops, claps. Food and drink are passed around.

In a mountain rainforest of the Congo, a Nyanga village hears once more the tale of its favorite hero—Mwindo, the one born walking, the one born talking . . .

1
The Son

In the village of Tubondo lived a great chief. His name was She-Mwindo.

One day he called together his seven wives and his counselors and all his people. He told them, "When a daughter marries, her family is paid a bride-price. But when a son marries, it is his family that pays it. So, all my children must be daughters. If any is a son, I will kill him."

The people were astonished. But they said nothing, for they were afraid of him.

Soon all the chief's seven wives became pregnant. The children of six wives arrived on the same day. They were all daughters. But the child of his favorite wife did not arrive.

The child that did not arrive was Mwindo. He was not ready to arrive.

At last he told himself, "I am ready. But I will not come out like other babies. I will come out through my mother's navel."

His mother lay in bed. He came out through her navel. He jumped down and ran around the room. In his hand was a *conga* flyswatter, with a handle of wood and a swatter of buffalo tail.

His mother cried out. "*Aieeeeeee!* What kind of child is this?"

The baby sang and danced and waved his conga.

> I am Mwindo,
> the one born walking,
> the one born talking.
> My father She-Mwindo does not want me.
> My father the chief wants to kill me.
> But what can he do against me?

She-Mwindo heard the noise. He went to the house of his favorite wife. He saw the boy and was full of rage. "What is this? Did I not say 'no sons'? Did I not say I would kill him?"

He threw his spear at the baby. Mwindo waved his conga. The spear fell short and stuck in the floor. Mwindo pulled it up. He broke it in two.

She-Mwindo cried out. "*Aieeeeeee!* What kind of child is this?"

Mwindo sang and danced and waved his conga.

> I am Mwindo,
> the one born walking,
> the one born talking.
> O my father, you do not want me.
> O my father, you try to kill me.
> But what can you do against me?

The chief rushed out. He called his counselors. "My favorite wife has given birth to a son. I cannot spear him. But I can bury him. Dig a grave and put him in."

The counselors said nothing. They dug a grave. They put Mwindo at the bottom. They threw in the dirt.

The day was done. Everyone went to sleep. The next morning, the chief woke up. He heard a song.

I am Mwindo,
the one born walking,
the one born talking.
My father does not want me.
My father tried to bury me.
But what can he do against me?

The chief rushed from his house. He went to the grave. It was all dug up. He went to the house of his favorite wife. The baby was on her lap.

She-Mwindo cried out. "*Aieeeeeee!* What kind of child is this?"

He went and called his counselors. "I cannot spear the child. I cannot bury him. But I can float him down the river. Make a drum and put him in."

The counselors said nothing. They cut a piece of log and hollowed it. They prepared two antelope hides. They placed the baby inside. They laced and pegged the hides.

The chief took the drum to the river. He threw it far out. He looked to see it float downstream.

The drum did not float downstream. It floated just where it was. The chief heard a song.

I am Mwindo,
the one born walking,
the one born talking.
O my father, you do not want me.
O my father, you send me downriver.
What is downriver?
Nothing for Mwindo!
What is upriver?
Something for Mwindo—

> my father's sister,
> my aunt Iyangura.
> My father does not want me,
> but my aunt will want me.
> Mwindo will not go downriver,
> Mwindo will go upriver.
> Mwindo goes where he wants to go.

The drum floated upstream. She-Mwindo cried out. "*Aieeeeeee!* What kind of child is this?" Then he said, "But now he's gone." He returned to the village.

Mwindo went upstream. He was going to Aunt Iyangura. He came near her village. He floated his drum to the bank.

The serving girls of Iyangura came to draw water. They saw the drum and heard a song.

> I am Mwindo,
> the one born walking,
> the one born talking.
> My father did not want me.
> My father tried to kill me.
> But Aunt Iyangura will want me.

The girls rushed to tell Iyangura. She came running. With a knife, she slashed open the drum. There was the baby with his conga. Iyangura was astonished. He shone like the rising sun.

Iyangura said, "What a fine boy is Mwindo! How could my brother reject him? Iyangura will not reject him!" She picked him up. She carried him to her house and cared for him.

2
The Battle

Mwindo grew up. A day went by, a week, a month, and he was grown. Then he said, "O my aunt, thank you for caring for me. Now I go to fight my father."

His aunt said, "What is this talk? Your father's village is huge. He has many men to fight for him. You cannot fight your father."

But Mwindo sang and danced and waved his conga.

> I am Mwindo,
> the one born walking,
> the one born talking.
> My father did not want me.
> My father tried to kill me.
> Now he must fight me.

His aunt said, "All right, then. But I will go with you. And let us first visit your mother's brothers, the blacksmiths. They will forge you, so no weapon can pierce you."

Mwindo and his aunt started off. Iyangura brought her servants and the musicians and drummers of her village. They all sang and danced as they went.

They reached the village of Mwindo's uncles, the blacksmiths. Mwindo said, "O my uncles, my father tried to kill me. Now I go to fight him. Forge me, so no weapon can pierce me."

His uncles stoked the fire. They took Mwindo apart in pieces—his arms, his legs, his trunk, his head. They put the pieces in the fire. They hammered them on the forge.

They put Mwindo back together. His body was like iron. No weapon could pierce it.

Mwindo said, "Now I go to fight my father."

His uncles told him, "The village of She-Mwindo is huge. He has many men to fight for him. Let us go and help you."

They started to his father's village. The uncles brought their servants and the musicians and drummers of their village. They all sang and danced as they went.

They came to the foot of the mountain, below the village of Tubondo. Iyangura said, "O my nephew, there are many of us. We have come a long way, singing and dancing. Now we are hungry. But we have no food! What can we do?"

Mwindo said, "O my aunt, you have fed me all my life. My father has not fed me. Now he will give us what he owes me."

Mwindo sang and danced and waved his conga.

> Bananas of my father, come to me.
> Beans of my father, come to me.
> Pumpkins of my father, come to me.
> Chickens of my father, come to me.
> Goats of my father, come to me.
> Pots of my father, come to me.
> Firewood of my father, come to me.
> Dishes of my father, come to me.

Up the mountain, She-Mwindo saw things rise up and fly away—his bananas, his beans, his pumpkins, his chickens, his goats, his pots, his firewood, his dishes. He cried out. "*Aieeeeeee!* What is this?"

The things flew down the mountain to Mwindo. Everyone had a great feast. No one was hungry.

Mwindo said, "Now I go to fight my father."

His uncles said, "Let us go there before you."

The uncles went up to the village with their weapons. They entered the gate. They said, "Fight, O men of Tubondo!"

The men of Tubondo fought. All the uncles died. Their bodies lay in the dust.

Down the mountain, Mwindo said, "Where are my uncles?"

Hawk flew down. "O Mwindo, all your uncles are dead. The men of Tubondo have killed them."

Mwindo sang and danced and waved his conga.

> I am Mwindo,
> the one born walking,
> the one born talking.
> My father did not want me.
> My father tried to kill me.
> He did not kill me,
> but he killed my uncles.
> Now he will fight Mwindo.
> Again he will try to kill me.
> But what can he do against me?

Mwindo danced up to the village. He had no weapon. He danced through the gate.

The chief said, "Who is this strange fellow? Should we kill him?"

Mwindo sang and danced and waved his conga.

> I am Mwindo,
> the one born walking,

the one born talking.
O my father, you did not want me.
O my father, you tried to kill me.
You did not kill me,
but you killed my uncles.
Now you will fight Mwindo.
Again you will try to kill me.
But what can you do against me?

She-Mwindo trembled. "O men of Tubondo, throw your spears! Shoot your arrows!"

The men of Tubondo threw their spears and shot their arrows. The spears and arrows struck Mwindo and bounced off. His body was like iron. No weapon could pierce it.

She-Mwindo cried out. "*Aieeeeeee!* What kind of man is this?" He ran away to his house.

Mwindo sang and danced and waved his conga.

O Lightning, look here.
O Lightning, be the judge.
Is my father right?
Is Mwindo right?
O Lightning, send your bolt.
Show who's right,
show who's wrong.

Lightning sent his bolt. It struck the men of Tubondo. The men died. Their bodies lay in the dust.

The chief saw from his house. He trembled and shook. "What a powerful man is Mwindo! What a mistake to reject him! But how can I now face him! He will kill me!"

Mwindo sang and danced and waved his conga.

Lightning looked here.
Lightning was the judge.
He showed who's right,
he showed who's wrong.

Iyangura came up to the village. She saw the bodies lying in the dust. "What is this? O my nephew, you came to fight your father. But now all these people are dead—your uncles and the men of Tubondo!"

Mwindo stopped dancing. He was sad to see everyone dead.

He went to one man. He swatted him with his conga—once, twice, three times. He said, "First you sleep, now you wake."

The man woke up. He said, "What a great man is Mwindo! What can anyone do against you?"

Mwindo went to all the men. He swatted them with his conga—once, twice, three times. "First you sleep, now you wake."

All the men woke up. All the men said, "What a great man is Mwindo! What can anyone do against you?"

Mwindo said, "Where is my father?"

Hawk flew down. "O Mwindo, your father ran out the other gate. He came to a *kikoka* fern. He pulled it up by the roots and crawled through the hole. Now he is underground, in the land of the gods. He goes to the village of their chief—Nyamurairi, god of fire."

Mwindo said, "I go to bring home my father."

Iyangura said, "What is this talk? No one can do this. Only the dead go there, and none return."

But Mwindo sang and danced and waved his conga.

I am Mwindo,
the one born walking,
the one born talking.
My father did not want me.
My father tried to kill me.
Now he runs away.
But how can he escape me?
My father goes to the gods.
Mwindo goes there too.
Mwindo goes where he wants to go.
The son will find his father.
The father will face his son.

3
The Gods

Hawk led them to the kikoka. Mwindo said, "O my aunt, good-bye. Wait for me till you see me." Everyone wept.

Mwindo pulled up the kikoka and crawled through the hole. He was underground, in the land of the gods. He started to the village of Nyamurairi. The land was cold and gray, without sun or moon or stars.

He came to the place where the women draw water. There was Kahindo, the chief god's daughter. Mwindo was astonished. She shone like the rising sun.

Kahindo saw him. "What a splendid young man is Mwindo! I welcome you." She embraced him a long time. She said, "What has brought you to the land of the gods?"

Mwindo said, "I come to bring home my father."

Kahindo said, "No one can do this. Only the dead come here, and none return."

He said, "I will do it."

She told him, "My father will try to trick you. He will offer you beer. You must say, 'Though I am your guest, shall I drink water that has passed through my host?' He will offer you porridge. You must say, 'Though I am your guest, shall I eat food that has passed through my host?' Say these things and you will be safe."

Mwindo went into the village. He came to the house of Nyamurairi, the chief. The god sat on a stool by the fire. He was an old man with a long beard. He smoked a clay pipe and wore a white goatskin. "Greetings, Mwindo. What has brought you to the land of the gods?"

Mwindo said, "I come to bring home my father."

The god said, "No one can do this. Only the dead come here, and none return. Your father cannot return. You too cannot return."

Mwindo sang and danced and waved his conga.

> I am Mwindo,
> the one born walking,
> the one born talking.
> My father went to the gods.
> Mwindo went there too.
> O god of fire,
> even you cannot stop me.
> O god of death,
> even you cannot hold me.
> What can you do against me?
> Mwindo goes where he wants to go.

The god said, "Is this so? We will see about it. But you have come far. You are thirsty. You must have beer." He held out a cup.

Mwindo said, "Though I am your guest, shall I drink water that has passed through my host?"

The god said, "You are right! But you have come far. You are hungry. You must have porridge." He held out a bowl.

Mwindo said, "Though I am your guest, shall I eat food that has passed through my host?"

The god was astonished. "What a clever young man is Mwindo! We must see more of his skill. At sunrise you will start a banana grove. By sundown you will bring ripe bananas. If you do, you can take home your father."

Mwindo spent the night in the house of Kahindo. At dawn, Nyamurairi came. He gave Mwindo a billhook knife and an ax and a bundle of banana shoots. He showed the place in the forest for the banana grove. He left him there.

Mwindo put the things down—the billhook, the ax, the banana shoots. He swatted the billhook with his conga—once, twice, three times. He said, "First you rest, now you work." The billhook jumped up. It cleared the brush from between the trees.

Mwindo swatted the ax—once, twice, three times. "First you rest, now you work." The ax jumped up. It cut the trees down.

Mwindo swatted the banana shoots—once, twice, three times. "First you rest, now you work." The shoots jumped up. They planted themselves and grew.

Mwindo lay down and rested. The banana trunks grew tall. They flowered. They bore fruit. The fruit ripened. The billhook cut it down.

Mwindo got up. He carried the bananas to Nyamurairi. The sun set.

The god was astonished. "What a clever young man is Mwindo! We must see more of his skill. Tomorrow you will gather honey from a certain tree. If you do, you can take home your father."

Mwindo spent the night in the house of Kahindo. At dawn, Nyamurairi came. He gave Mwindo a torch and an ax and a calabash. He showed him the honey tree. He left him there.

Mwindo climbed the tree. With the torch, he smoked out the bees. With the ax, he chopped an opening. But he could not reach the honey.

Mwindo climbed down. He sang and danced and waved his conga.

> O Lightning, look here.
> O Lightning, be the judge.
> Is the god right?
> Is Mwindo right?
> Without your bolt,
> there is no honey.
> Without honey,
> there is no father.
> O Lightning, send your bolt.
> Show who's right,
> show who's wrong.

Lightning sent his bolt. It split the tree. Mwindo climbed up and reached the honey. He put it in the calabash. He brought it to Nyamurairi.

The god was astonished. "What a clever young man is Mwindo! We must reward his skill. O Mwindo, take this gift—my belt of cowrie shells."

Nyamurairi took off his belt. He threw it at Mwindo. It wrapped itself around him. It squeezed him. Mwindo could not pull it off. Mwindo could not breathe. He dropped his conga. He fell to the ground. He died. His body lay in the dust.

The god laughed. "What a foolish boaster is Mwindo! Did the god of fire not stop him? Did the god of death not hold him?"

He saw the conga rise up. He cried out. "*Aieeeeeee!* What is this?"

The conga swatted the belt—once, twice, three times. The belt dropped away. The conga swatted Mwindo—once, twice, three times. Mwindo breathed. He rose and took the conga.

Mwindo picked up the belt. He threw it at Nyamurairi. It wrapped itself around him. It squeezed him. The god could not pull it off. The god could not breathe. He fell to the ground. He died. His body lay in the dust.

Mwindo sang and danced and waved his conga,

> I am Mwindo,
> the one born walking,
> the one born talking.
> My father went to the gods.
> Mwindo went there too.
> The god of fire tried to stop me,
> but Mwindo stopped the god.
> The god of death tried to hold me,
> but Mwindo held the god.
> What could he do against me?
> Mwindo goes where he wants to go.
> The son will find his father.
> The father will face his son.

Kahindo came there. She saw the god lying in the dust. "What is this? O Mwindo, you came to bring home your father. But now my father is dead!"

Mwindo stopped dancing. He was sad to see Nyamurairi dead. He swatted him with his conga—once, twice, three times. "First you sleep, now you wake."

Nyamurairi woke. He said, "What a great man is Mwindo! What can anyone do against you? Take home your father."

Mwindo said, "Where is he?"

Hawk flew down. "O Mwindo, your father runs away again!"

4
The Father

Mwindo ran from the village of Nyamurairi. He saw his father. His father ran fast. Mwindo ran faster. Mwindo caught his father. They fell to the ground.

She-Mwindo trembled and shook and quaked. He said, "Will you kill me?"

Mwindo said, "No, I will not kill you."

"Will you hurt me?"

"No, I will not hurt you."

"Will you take what is mine?"

"No, I will not take what is yours."

"Then what do you want with me?"

Mwindo said, "A father cannot be a father without a son, and a son cannot be a son without a father. You must be my father so I can be your son."

She-Mwindo was astonished. "What a wise young man is Mwindo! What a mistake to reject him! No longer will She-Mwindo reject him. I will be your father, and you will be my son."

Mwindo sang and danced and waved his conga.

> I am Mwindo,
> the one born walking,
> the one born talking.
> O my father, you did not want me.
> O my father, you tried to spear me.
> You tried to bury me.

You tried to send me downriver.
You set your men against me.
Then you ran away from me.
But how could you escape me?
The son found his father.
The father faced his son.
Now you are truly my father.
Now I am truly your son.
She-Mwindo has a son!
Mwindo has a father!

Mwindo brought his father to the kikoka. They crawled through the hole, up to the land of the living. Everyone was waiting for them—Iyangura, the counselors, the seven wives of the chief, all the people of Tubondo. Everyone was astonished and happy.

She-Mwindo told them, "This I have learned: A man must not value only a daughter or only a son. Each is a blessing of its own. What a wonderful son is Mwindo!"

* * *

When She-Mwindo grew old and died, Mwindo became chief. He was very famous. To this day, people tell of him—the one born walking, the one born talking.

Mwindo!

Author Online!

For special features and more stories,
visit Aaron Shepard at

www.aaronshep.com

About the Story

The Mwindo epic comes from the Nyanga, one of the Bantu-speaking peoples that live in the mountainous rainforests in the east of the Congo. (A former name of the Congo was Zaire). In the 1950s, when the epic was collected, the Nyanga numbered about 27,000. Traditionally, they are governed by chiefs, each one ruling over several villages.

The Nyanga themselves have no written version of the Mwindo epic, so it has never reached a standardized form. Of the four versions transcribed and published by outsiders, no two are even nearly the same—and no doubt there are many other distinct versions.

The epic is performed as simple entertainment by amateur bards. The bards' performance includes song and dance, accompanied by drummers and other musicians. Only a portion of the epic is performed at a time, as a complete performance would take too long.

Following are notes on particular elements of the story.

Mwindo. The Nyanga do not seem to claim Mwindo as a historical figure, and there is no reason to believe he was one. The name itself has no remembered meaning, but it is now commonly given to a son born after many daughters.

She-Mwindo. The name means "father of Mwindo"—so, of course, it could not really have been his name when the story starts!

Bride-price. In most of Africa—and in many other cultures worldwide—it is the custom for a groom and his family to send a substantial wedding gift to the family of the bride. This is basically the reverse form of "dowry," a custom that is common elsewhere. Names for the gift include "wooing present," "bride-price," and "bride-wealth." Where this is practiced, the birth of many sons can impoverish a family, while the birth of many daughters can enrich it.

Conga. This is a flyswatter with a scepter-like handle of wood. The swatter attached at the top can be leaves, an antelope tail, or, as in this story, the tail of a Cape buffalo. A conga is included in the regalia of a chief, and so signifies here the destiny of Mwindo.

Lightning. To the Nyanga, Lightning is a god who may be entreated to intervene in human affairs by sending down his bolts. He is the only Nyanga god who lives in the sky. How his bolts can reach underground to the land of the gods is a mystery.

Land of the gods. The Nyanga say the gods live in their own land underground, where the dead also go. Except for being cold and dreary, it is much like the land of the Nyanga.

Nyamurairi. The gods' own chief is Nyamurairi. He is the god of fire, and also the ultimate giver of life and death. His home village is where the dead reside.

Kahindo. This goddess, who appears here as Nyamurairi's daughter, is sometimes identified with Kahombo, the goddess of fortune.

Bananas, porridge. The staple food of the Nyanga is the banana—not the sweet fruit known to most of us, but the plantain, a starchy fruit. Among the Nyanga, it is dried, pounded, ground into a flour, and cooked as a porridge.

Though this retelling is in my own words, I've done my best to retain the flavor of the original. Sources for the retelling were:

The Mwindo Epic: From the Banyanga (Congo Republic), edited and translated by Daniel Biebuyck and Kahombo C. Mateene, University of California Press, Berkeley and Los Angeles, 1969. (*Banyanga* means "the Nyanga people.")
Hero and Chief: Epic Literature from the Banyanga, Zaire Republic, Daniel P. Biebuyck, University of California Press, Berkeley, Los Angeles, and London, 1978.

For special features, please visit www.aaronshep.com.

Aaron Shepard

Aaron Shepard is the award-winning author of *The Sea King's Daughter, The Baker's Dozen,* and many more children's books from publishers large and small. His stories also appear often in *Cricket* and in Australia's *School Magazine.* Visit him at www.aaronshep.com.

CPSIA information can be obtained
at www.ICGtesting.com
Printed in the USA
LVOW08s1125020717

540115LV00002B/241/P